Giggle, Giggle, Quack

ARTIST'S NOTE

For this book I did brush drawings using Winsor & Newton lamp black watercolor on tracing paper. I then had the drawings photocopied onto one-ply Strathmore kid finish watercolor paper and applied watercolor washes to the black drawings. The advantage to this method is that I can get as many copies on the watercolor paper as I want, and I can experiment with the color, choosing the finishes that I like the best.

SIMON & SCHUSTER BOOKS FOR YOUNG READERS
An imprint of Simon & Schuster Children's Publishing Division,
1230 Avenue of the Americas, New York, New York 10020.
Text copyright © 2002 by Doreen Cronin. Illustrations copyright © 2002 by Betsy Lewin.
All rights reserved, including the right of reproduction in whole or in part in any form.
SIMON & SCHUSTER BOOKS FOR YOUNG READERS is a trademark of Simon & Schuster.
Book design by Anahid Hamparian. The text of this book is set in 30-point Filosofia Bold. Printed in Mexico
4 6 8 10 9 7 5 3

Library of Congress Cataloging-in-Publication Data
Cronin, Doreen. Giggle, giggle, quack /
by Doreen Cronin ; illustrated by Betsy Lewin. —1st ed.
p. cm.
Summary: When Farmer Brown goes on vacation, leaving his brother Bob in charge,
Duck makes trouble by changing all the instructions to notes the animals like much better.
ISBN 0-689-84506-5
[1. Ducks—Fiction. 2. Domestic animals—Fiction.] I. Lewin, Betsy, ill. II. Title.
PZ7.C88135 Gi 2002 [E]—dc21 2001032201

For Andrew
—D. C.

For Rosanne Lauer
—B. L.

Giggle, Giggle, Quack

by Doreen Cronin   pictures by Betsy Lewin

Simon & Schuster Books for Young Readers

New York London Toronto Sydney Singapore

Farmer Brown was going on vacation. He left his brother, Bob, in charge of the animals.

"I wrote everything down for you.
Just follow my instructions and
everything will be fine. But keep
an eye on Duck. He's trouble."

Farmer Brown thought he heard
giggles and snickers as he drove
away, but he couldn't be sure.

Bob gave Duck a good long stare and went inside.
He read the first note:

Giggle, giggle, cluck.

Twenty-nine minutes later
there was hot pizza in the barn.

before he went to bed.
Everything was just fine.

Wednesday is bath day for the pigs.
Wash them with my favorite bubble bath and dry them off with my good towels.
Remember, they have very sensitive skin.

Giggle, giggle, oink.

Bob had all the pigs washed in no time.

Farmer Brown called home on Wednesday night to check in. "Did you feed the animals like I wrote in the note?" he asked.

"Done," replied Bob, counting seven empty pizza boxes.

"Did you see my note about the pigs?"
"All taken care of," said Bob proudly.

"Are you keeping a very close eye on Duck?" he asked.

Bob gave Duck a good long stare. Duck was too busy sharpening his pencil to notice.

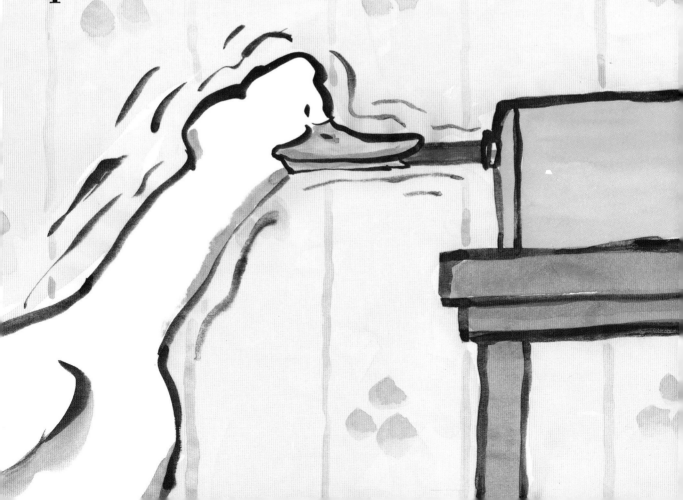

"Just keep him in the house," ordered Farmer Brown. "He's a bad influence on the cows."

Giggle, giggle, moo, giggle, oink, giggle, quack.

Thursday night is movie night. It's the cows' turn to pick.

Giggle, giggle, moo.

Bob was in the kitchen, popping corn. Just as the animals settled in to watch THE SOUND OF MOOSIC, the phone rang.

The only thing Farmer Brown heard on the other end was:

"Giggle, giggle, quack, giggle, moo, giggle, oink...."

UH-OH.

"DUCK!" screamed Farmer Brown.